THE STORY OF
THE LOCKDOWN

BY DEBORAH HALTER
with illustrations by IAN WARD

OWN BOOKS

GIVING ALL CHILDREN
THE ENJOYMENT OF BOOKS

www.ownbooks.co.uk

APS Books
YORKSHIRE

Bon Bon is a little lamb, her fleece as white as snow.
When she lost her Mummy, she had nowhere to go.

One day whilst playing in a field,
Max and Mimi suddenly squealed!

A little lamb was all alone.
"Oh no!" they cried, "let's take her home."

Inside they went and ran a bath,
bubbles everywhere, what a laugh!

Bon Bon splashed and enjoyed the rub,
having lots of fun in the bath tub!

Out she came looking fluffy and clean,
the cutest lamb they had ever seen!

On the doorstep the family clapped out loud,
For the NHS heroes, they were all so proud.

After milk, it was time for bed,
Bon Bon laid down her curly head.

In the morning when Bon Bon awoke,
to Mimi's surprise the little lamb spoke!

"Where is my mummy?" Bon Bon cried,
"We will help you find her!" the children replied.

They looked in the chicken coop, behind a sack.

"I'll help you look" clucked Chester the chicken,

jumping up on Bon Bon's back.

And off they went, Max, Mimi, Bon Bon and Chester.

They looked in the stable, and under the table,
they looked in the straw and behind the door.

They saw Jess the Horse, nibbling her hay.
"I'll help you look!" they heard her neigh.

And off they went, Max, Mimi,
Bon Bon, Chester and Jess.

They went into the kennel, and saw a dog called Beau.
"I'll help you look!" he woofed. "We will search high and low!"

And off they went, Max, Mimi,
Bon Bon, Chester, Jess and Beau.

They went into a field and saw billy goats graze.
"We will help you too, or you will be searching for days!"

And off they went, Max, Mimi, Bon Bon,
Chester, Jess, Beau and the billy goats.

They skipped over the bridge, above the stream,
Suddenly, Max let out a scream!
A flock of sheep appeared in view,
A ewe jumped out and Bon Bon knew

"My Mummy!" she bleated and ran to her side.
She thanked the gang and exclaimed "I've arrived!"

Off she skipped to pastures new.
"Goodbye and good luck!" chanted her crew.

THE END

The real lockdown lamb
who couldn't find her Mummy!